MANGO HILL
by
diana hansen-young

Published by ISLAND HERITAGE
A Division of The Madden Corporation

For Heidi and Thekla
©1988 by Diana Hansen-Young
P.O. Box 1159
Kaneohe, Hawaii 96744
(808) 239-4952

Please address orders to:
Island Heritage
99-880 Iwaena Street
Aiea, Hawaii 96701
ISBN 0-89610-150-9

MANGO HILL

by
Diana Hansen-Young

Once upon a time there was a very special mouse who lived in the roots of a mango tree high on a hill in Kahaluu, on the island of Oahu.

Her former home had been with a professor, whose wife discovered her inside a hollowed-out art book.

"Get rid of that mouse!" she screamed, waving the shredded, pageless book at the professor.

A firm believer in non-violence, the professor released the mouse in the countryside, near a hill covered with mango, lychee and java plum trees.

The mouse called her new home Mango Hill. She fixed up a small burrow beneath the roots of the largest mango tree. Her days were spent gathering food, or playing in the nearby stream.

But, being a smart, sociable mouse with artistic talent, she longed for good friends and sparkling conversation.

The only other residents of the hill were the noisy and quarrelsome mynah birds, and the dangerous, evil centipedes, who lived under the lychee trees.

As time passed she grew lonely and longed for a family or friends. . . someone to share her life with on Mango Hill.

One night, she heard loud rumbling noises across the valley.

It must be New Year's Eve, she thought, when the Chinese beetles usually sent up a wild display of fireworks.

But instead of fireworks, huge drops of water splashed down against the burrow, followed by fierce rain and strong winds! Bolts of lightning shook the very roots of her mango tree!

It was the worse storm she had ever seen.

Soon the burrow was completely flooded. Frightened, she rushed from her ruined home and took refuge high in the tree branches, where she crouched, shivering in the rain, until morning.

With the dawn, she was able to see the damage the storm had done.
Broken tree branches lay in the mud, and water covered the ground.
But there was something else! Something moving! Crawling weakly
up the hill were three little muddy balls of fur!

Quickly she raced to the breadfruit tree, plucked a large, shiny leaf, and scampered down the hill. She rolled the muddy animals onto the leaf, and tugged them up the hill, where she piled on dry leaves to keep them warm.

That night, exhausted after cleaning out her burrow, she arranged her new family around her and snuggled up close.

She fell asleep even before her ears hit the soft, mossy pillow.

She was awakened by hungry meowing.

She stared in amazement at what the storm had brought her.

Three kittens?! No! — Two! The third ball of fur shook itself, and two long floppy ears became unstuck from the dried mud. It was a small bunny!

The tiny animals looked at her hopefully.

"I'm not your mother," she said to them. "But I guess I'm all the family you've got, so I'll have to do."

The little kittens meowed.

"Hungry?" she asked. "There's plenty of fruit to eat. Come along and I'll show you."

Her new family bounced along behind her to the top of Mango Hill. She stopped, and looked at the scruffy little collection of animals. She felt very motherly, and happy. She swept her paw across the wide expanse of land.

"Welcome to Mango Hill," she said grandly. "Your new home!"

The mouse enjoyed raising her new family.

It was easy to show the bunny where to find choice grass and fruit. She had a tough time teaching the little kittens to eat mangos when they seemed to prefer beetles and bugs. One of them developed a taste for java plums, and as the kitten grew older, her fur turned a delicate purple.

Once in a while, the gray mouse saw a hungry look from the larger kitten. This lip-licking worried her a little, and she decided it was time to begin their education.

Lessons began with gratitude, the morality of not biting the hand that fed them, and self-confidence.

"You can be anything you want to be," she told them.

"Except thin," snickered the kittens, eyeing the bunny, whose increasing roundness wa the subject of many jokes.

Mouse stopped the teasing, and ended the lesson, as always, with a serious warning: "Stay away from the lychee trees. That's where the Centipede King lives! The Pedes are evil and dangerous! They'll bite you just for the fun of it!"

The bunny shivered delicately at the thought of the evil centipedes. That night she snuggled extra close to the gray mouse.

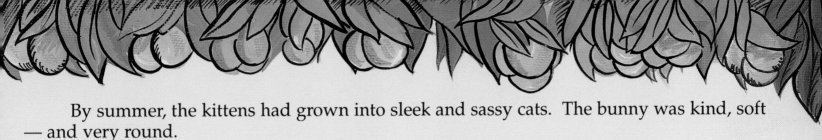

By summer, the kittens had grown into sleek and sassy cats. The bunny was kind, soft — and very round.

One morning, in the middle of quarreling, teasing, unkind plumpness remarks, and a lot of complaining about nothing to do, they suddenly heard noises down by the road.

They ran out of their burrow in time to see a woman with yellow hair and a man with black hair and mustache pulling up in a car.

Two little girls piled out and ran, laughing and shouting, across Mango Hill.

"This is it," they heard the woman say. "It's perfect! Look at these trees! We'll call it Mango Hill!"

"That was my idea first," thought Mouse, herding her family back inside the burrow until the humans were gone.

That night, she sat up late, worrying, deeply troubled by what she'd heard. Would her family be broken up? Would their life change? What would happen to them now?

And what would happen to Mango Hill?

By fall, her worse fears had come true.

Bulldozers had cleared much of the hill. Cement foundations were poured, and work-men built a new house.

"Why do we have to share Mango Hill?" pouted the cats, sulking around. "We were here first."

"Just be grateful they didn't knock down our tree," the bunny said.

"Oh just be quiet," hissed the white cat. "You're always so — so — foolishly grateful!"

"Gratitude has its downside," said the purple cat. The brief image of a mouse burger flashed in front of her, but her sense of morality, which had been drilled into her, pushed the tasty, but forbidden, thought from her mind.

The new family soon moved into their new house on Mango Hill.

Every night, there were the sounds of children playing, music, and fun coming from the house which was shaped like a castle, with two turrets and arched windows.

The lights stayed on far into the night.

What was going on?

Mouse could no longer contain her curiosity.

"I'm going in," she announced bravely. She kissed her family goodbye. "If I don't come back — well — I love you all!"

They waited for what seemed like hours for the mouse to return. They huddled together, like a true family, leaning on each other for support. Even the larger cat was scared. What if something horrible happened? She decided to apologize.

"I'm sorry for my fat bunny jokes," she began, but just then there was a noise outside!

Mouse was home!

"Follow me!" Mouse said excitedly. "I finally found a way in! We'll go through the dryer vent! They leave the dryer door open! Come on! You have to see this for yourselves!"

Around the side of the house they ran, leaping easily into the dryer vent — all except bunny, who had a tough time squeezing through the opening because of her general state of roundness.

They followed Mouse through the dryer, down a long, dark hallway, across a very soft rug and through the big kitchen — where a plate of ribs sat unattended on the counter.

The cats stopped in awe, but the mouse urged them onwards. "Follow me," she called.

She led them to another room, filled with jars, brushes and paints.

"Look!" she said excitedly. "The woman is an ARTIST!"

"Big deal," said the white cat, thinking of the ribs in the kitchen.

"Look at these beautiful paintings!" Mouse said, pointing around the studio. "Aren't they wonderful?"

"Boring," yawned the purple cat, also thinking of the ribs.

The bunny read the title of a painting that leaned against the wall. "Hibiscus Hat," she said aloud. "I've always wanted to look like that. Elegant, thin, and well-dressed."

"Why, you can," said the mouse. "You just need a dress and hat!"

The bunny looked at her in astonishment. "I think you're right," she said slowly. "I CAN be anything I want to be!"

"I'll make you a dress and a hat just like that," Mouse promised.

"Oh, wow," laughed the purple cat meanly. "Then you'll look dumber and fatter."

"Stop it!" said Mouse. She turned to the bunny, whose eyes were beginning to fill with tears. "From now on, your name will be — Hibiscus Bunny!" Hibiscus Bunny smiled happily.

The purple cat started to sneer, but the white cat stopped her.

"Look at this painting." She read the back. "Ohana: Two Sisters."

"Ohana is family," said Mouse. "And you're sisters. From now on, we'll call you the Ohana Cats!"

"How stupid," said the purple cat sarcastically, turning up her nose. But then she started to think how nice she might look.

"Would you make me a muumuu?" she asked the Mouse. "And trim it in java plum purple?"

"I'll make you all dresses," exclaimed Mouse. "Just like these."
"But what about you?" asked Hibiscus Bunny. "Who will you be?"
The mouse had her eye on the painting on the easel.
"Seated Halau Dancer," she read on the back. It looked just like her.
"From now on," she said, with a secret smile, "I'll be Halau Mouse!"

Suddenly a woman's voice floated down from upstairs.

"I'm going to the kitchen," the human said. "I forgot to put away the leftover ribs."

Halau Mouse saw two mismatched red and yellow socks coming down the stairs.

"It's the artist woman," Mouse squeaked frantically. "Quick! Everybody out!"

Back across the rug, down the hallway and through the kitchen they ran. The Ohana cats snatched a few ribs as they passed and headed toward the dryer vent, and safety.

Back in their burrow, the cats munched on ribs while they all talked about the exciting evening in the wonderful new house.

Long after the cats were asleep, and Hibiscus Bunny was dreaming about a soft rug, Halau Mouse lay awake in bed, thinking of all the wonderful paints and brushes she had seen — all just waiting for her!

As she had promised, Halau Mouse cut paper-tree bark and stitched new muumuus carefully. She wove choice grasses for Hibiscus Bunny's new hat, and dyed the muumuus for the Ohana Cats with the juice from the java plum berries they collected.

Late at night, the four animals, dressed in their finery, would visit the house. The cats would dine on leftovers, and Hibiscus Bunny would relax and doze on the rug.

But Halau Mouse always went directly to the studio to see what the artist woman had painted that day.

Halau Mouse studied the paintings, the jars of acrylic paint and brushes. A few times she crept in alone to sit quietly in a corner and watch the artist work.

Finally, one night, when the house was dark and quiet, she could no longer resist temptation.

She picked up a brush, mixed some green paint, and added a few leaves to a maile lei the artist had painted on a white dress.

A thrill ran through her from head to toe!

She knew then that she was born to paint!

From then on, she grew bolder, adding flowers and hats. On one occasion, she even painted a small gecko into the green maile leaves, something that she felt enhanced the overall ambiance of the painting.

The animals loved the house on Mango Hill.

They thought of it as theirs, and the family as their own.

Halau Mouse began taking responsibility for the artist's paintings, often staying up late to finish what the artist had been too tired to complete.

The feeling that they belonged made it all the more shocking when they noticed more and more centipedes creeping into the house.

Once, Hibiscus Bunny was nearly bitten on the rug, and the Ohana cats had a knock-down drag-out fight with a couple of old Pedes who were carrying food away from the kitchen.

"Something is going on," said Halau Mouse. "And I intend to find out what."

"How?" whispered Hibiscus Bunny.

"Tonight I will visit the lychee trees."

There was stunned silence. Hibiscus Bunny shivered. "Do you have to?" she asked.

"Yes," said Halau Mouse, with a courage she did not feel. "This is our family. If the centipedes are up to something, it's up to us to stop them."

Halau Mouse wrapped herself with dead, dark leaves and smeared her paws and ears with dirt.

"Why are you doing that?" her family asked, huddled together.

"Camoflage," said Halau Mouse, who remembered shredding a military book long ago at the professor's house. "This way they can't see me."

She seemed brave, but inside, her stomach churned.

She took a deep breath, kissed her family, and vanished into the night.

Mango Hill suddenly seemed forbidding and dangerous.

The lychee trees swayed ominously in the moonlight. Under them, Halau Mouse heard the hissing and clicking of the ugly insects. She crept closer, all of her senses alert and tingling.

It was a council of war! Thousands of centipedes were gathered around the Centipede King! Moonlight shone on their shiny, armoured backs as their mandibles glistened beneath their buggy eyes.

The C'Pede King's cruel voice clicked its horrible words: "We take the house at midnight! It's warm, it has food — everything we need! But we must get rid of the humans!"

The army of Pedes cheered.

"This is the plan," the King continued. "We go in under the studio door, and up the stairs! Then, we split up — half to the adults, half to the kids. Hit them on their feet! Everyone! Take a bite! I want them covered with bites! And then — the house is ours!"

Centipede cheers filled the night.

Halau Mouse listened in horror. She looked up at the moon.

Only an hour till midnight! She had no time to lose!

Back in the burrow, Halau Mouse furiously drew a diagram in the dirt. "They'll come in under the studio door," she said. "Here's what we'll do."

She explained the plan.

"Whatever happens," she said, "don't let the centipedes up the stairs! If they get to the family — They'll die! It's up to us to protect them!"

"I'm scared," said Hibiscus Bunny in a low voice.

"We're all scared," said Halau Mouse. "But sometimes we have to do what we have to do — scared or not! Now let's go! Battle stations everyone!"

In the house, the family slept peacefully, unaware of the Pede's evil plans.

Downstairs in the studio, Halau Mouse moved everyone into position. She opened the jars of paint, handed everyone brushes and prepared their defenses.

The clock struck midnight!

"Now," said Halau Mouse. "Quiet everyone!" She surveyed the room. "We're ready. Let the centipedes come!"

A few seconds past midnight, brown shapes slithered under the door.

Hidden behind the paint jars, the animals looked at Halau Mouse, but she shook her head: No! Wait!

Soon the floor was covered with speeding Pedes, their millions of feet marching toward the stairs. "NOW!" shouted Halau Mouse.

"TAKE THAT!!" screamed Hibiscus Bunny, tipping over a row of open paint jars.

"AND THAT!!" cried Ohana Cats, emptying gallon tubs of acrylic on the centipedes.

Halau Mouse urged them on, waving a jumbo bristle brush in the air. "More paint! Faster! Turn them all over!"

Jars of pink, orange and green poured over the centipedes. They were trapped! They could not reach the stairs! A second volley of hand-mixed paints splashed over them!

"Retreat!" yelled a Pede, and, covered in pastel purples, he headed for the door.

The studio was a strange, colorful sea of sticky pink, purple and peach paint as pastel centipedes struggled toward the exit.

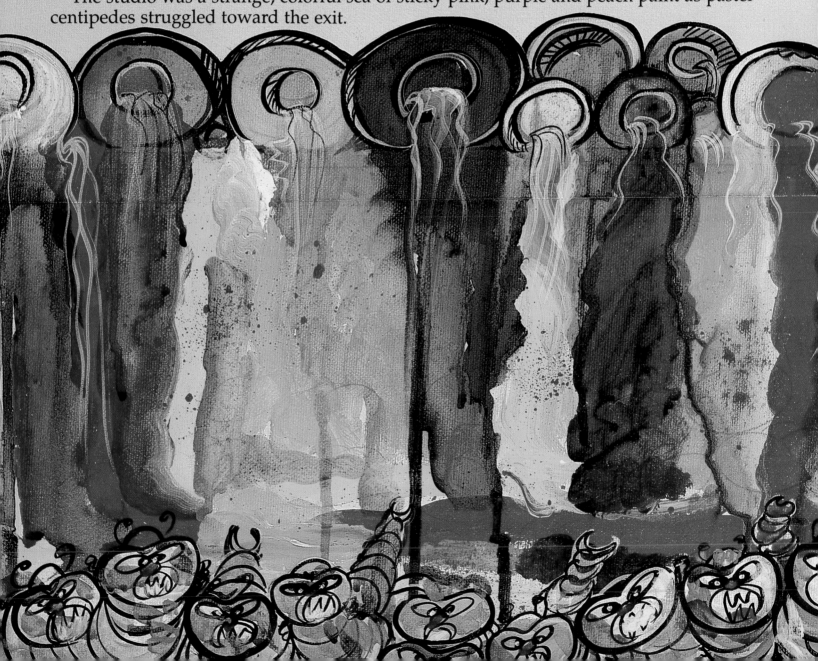

Suddenly, Halau Mouse saw the evil C'Pede King, covered with dusty rose paint, grinning from mandible to mandible.

He had escaped the sea of paint, and was headed toward the stairs!

With the jumbo brush in her teeth, Halau Mouse ran after him.

He sensed her behind him, and turned.

"You can't save them now," he snarled. "They're mine!"

Poison dripped from his jaws as he slithered toward the littlest girl's bedroom!

Faster than she had ever run in her life, Halau Mouse raced into the bedroom after the Centipede King.

Wham! She brought the jumbo brush down on his armoured body.

Wham!

She hit him again, just before his poisonous mandibles closed over a soft, chubby toe.

He turned on Halau Mouse, and lashed out with his tail.

Slam!

Fearlessly, she landed another heavy blow with her brush!

Wham!

The C'Pede King realized he had met his match. He slithered to the window.

"I'll be back," he hissed — and vanished into the night!

Halau Mouse drew a deep breath. Her hands were shaking — and then she remembered her family, downstairs!

Hibiscus Bunny and Ohana Cats let out a cheer when they saw that Halau Mouse was safe!

She looked around her. Every last jar of paint was empty, and the centipedes were gone!

They had done it! They had saved their family, and the house!

Suddenly, they heard a human noise from the stairway.

Their eyes traveled up — past two large feet — one in a red sock, and one in yellow — up to the shocked face of the artist who let out a big scream when she saw her studio.

Halau Mouse and her family stood frozen with fear. The woman looked out the glass studio doors, where thousands of pastel centipedes were limping away from the house. She looked at the paint-covered floor and the empty jars. Her eyes traveled out to the retreating Pedes, and back to the animals.

She finally understood what had happened.

"Why, you saved our lives!" she exclaimed.

She leaned over and looked closely at Halau Mouse, who still had the jumbo bristle brush in her paws.

Their eyes met.

"Are you the mouse that's been painting in my house?" she asked.

Halau Mouse tried to say something, but all that came out was a little squeak.

"Thank you," said the artist. "You've saved our lives. How can I ever thank you? For as long as you live on Mango Hill, you're welcome here. My house is your house."

But it was all too much for the animals. They leaped down, scrambled over the mismatched socks, skidded down the hallway, and threw themselves out the dryer vent towards the safety of the burrow.

It took a few days for them to really believe what the artist had told them.

"I think she MEANT it," said Hibiscus Bunny, thinking of the soft rug.

"No human would REALLY share their house, said the Ohana Cats, hoping against hope that it was really true.

"I think it's gratitude," said Halau Mouse.

So, they held a vote, and the decision was unanimous: they would return to the house and see if the artist meant what she said.

Once inside the house, they stopped in happy surprise.

On the kitchen counter, there were fresh carrots, catfood, a bowl of milk, and a plastic serving tray with French cheese and crackers.

They all looked at each other happily.

"That's gratitude for you," said the Ohana Cats, noisely lapping at the milk.

Hibiscus Bunny took her carrots into the living room to relax on the rug.

The studio was clean and neat. No trace remained of the terrible centipede war that had been fought there.

An unfinished canvas sat on the easel.

There was a note propped up against some new jars of paint.

"Go easy on the pink," the note read. "This painting needs strong peach flowers."

Eating her gourmet cheese and mixing her colors, Halau Mouse realized she was finally and truly happy.

She had her family, her friends — and besides, she could finally do what she was born to do . . . paint!